# CLAUDE

## in the City

ALEX T. SMITH

This is Claude.

Say hello, Claude.

Claude is a dog.
Claude is a small dog.
Claude is a small,
plump dog.

Claude is a small, plump dog
who wears a beret and a
lovely red jumper.

Beret

Lovely jumper

5

Claude lives in a house with Mr
and Mrs Shinyshoes.

Here they are now.

Claude also lives with his best friend, Sir Bobblysock.

Sir Bobblysock is both a sock and quite bobbly.

He is grubby and smells a bit like cheese.

Every morning, after breakfast, Mr and Mrs Shinyshoes put on their shiny shoes and their warm coats.

Claude watches them from his bed.

He watches them with one beady eye open and one beady eye closed, like this:

Or sometimes like this:

'Be a good boy, Claude!'
says Mr Shinyshoes.

'We'll be back soon!' says Mrs
Shinyshoes.

And off they go to work.

As soon as the door has closed
behind them, Claude opens both
beady eyes. He takes his beret out
from underneath his pillow and
pops it on his head.

Then he decides what
adventure he is going
to have that day.

12

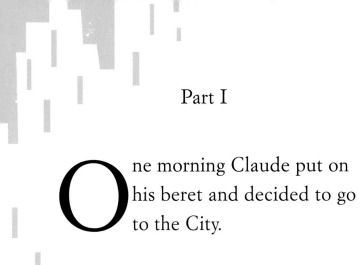

## Part I

One morning Claude put on his beret and decided to go to the City.

'I think I will go to the City,' he said, and he did.

Sir Bobblysock came too, as he didn't have anything else planned that day.

Claude had never been to the City before. He couldn't believe how tall all the buildings were. They stretched right up into the air and some of them disappeared into the clouds.

Sir Bobblysock was glad that it wasn't him who had to clean the windows.

The city was big and bright and very, very busy. There was so much to do!

First, Claude and Sir Bobblysock
went for a walk. They walked down
one long road and up another.

Everybody seemed very friendly!

Cars peeped their horns and some drivers shouted out to them.

But it was too noisy for Claude to hear what they were saying. Sir Bobblysock was slightly deaf in one ear so he was no help at all.

Next, they went to look at
the pigeons. There were lots
of pigeons in the city.

Claude looked at them very
closely and from every angle.

He looked:

*secretly

*shyly

*and as if he was trying
not to look at them at all.

Claude decided
that he liked
pigeons
very much
indeed!

19

By eleven o'clock Claude was feeling a little bit thirsty so he went to a fancy café with Sir Bobblysock.

Claude ordered a large hot chocolate with marshmallows and a straw.

Sir Bobblysock ordered a big, fruity cocktail which looked more like a plant pot!

Claude's drink was delicious and he drank every drop. Sir Bobblysock wasn't sure where to start...

Now it was time to go shopping!

Claude was amazed that there were so many different sorts of shops.

There were:
    *Shoe shops
    *Loo shops
    *Chip shops
    *Chop shops
    (which were really butcher's shops).

23

And there were even shops selling
the most curious contraptions
Claude had ever seen.

Then Sir Bobblysock discovered the
best shop in the world.

Ever.

Claude hurried inside. And bought
a beret in every colour and every
pattern.

Betty's Beret BOUTIQUE

That was an awful
lot of berets.

As they were setting off to find
some lunch, Claude spotted a very
interesting building.

It had lots of steps, some big pillars
at the front and it was exactly the
same colour as juicy bones. Juicy
bones happened to be Claude's
favourite things, after Sir
Bobblysock and his beret.

30

ART GALL

So Claude and Sir Bobblysock went inside. A helpful person sitting behind a big desk told them the building was an art gallery.

32

'Here is a guide,' she said helpfully, and handed Claude a guidebook. 'It tells you what is in each room.'

Claude said "thank you", left his boxes with her and set off with Sir Bobblysock.

He really liked looking at things and wanted to start straight away.

The first room Claude and Sir Bobblysock went into was full of sculptures.

Claude discovered sculptures were bits of art that weren't in frames and you could walk around, but absolutely not touch at all.

Claude was very interested. Some sculptures were

*enormous

\*titchy

\*very rude indeed.

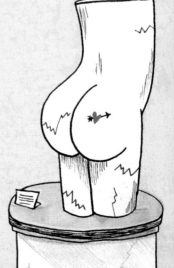

Claude looked at
his guidebook.

It said: Go into
the next room.

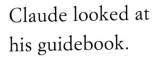

So he did.

On the walls were lots of
pictures in swirly frames.

Claude and Sir Bobblysock
sat down on a handy bench
and looked at them.

Some of the paintings showed people standing around and pointing at things that weren't there. Claude thought this was a little bit silly.

Some of the paintings had dogs in them, which made Claude happy. But none of them were wearing a beret...

38

'Let's go and have some lunch,' said
Claude to Sir Bobblysock. 'I could
just eat a juicy bone baguette!'

Claude collected his boxes
of berets and they set
off to find a café.

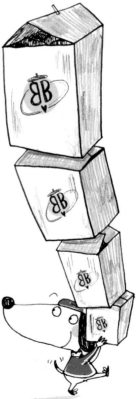

39

Suddenly a naughty robber in a striped jumper and a mask came running past them, carrying one of the sculptures.

Two guards were running after her.

Claude's paws were so full of boxes and his brain full of juicy bone baguette that he did not see her.

The robber did not see Claude and
all his boxes...

# BUMP!

# CRASH!

# WALLOP!

Berets exploded everywhere.

The robber fell to the ground.

The sculpture went flying through the air.

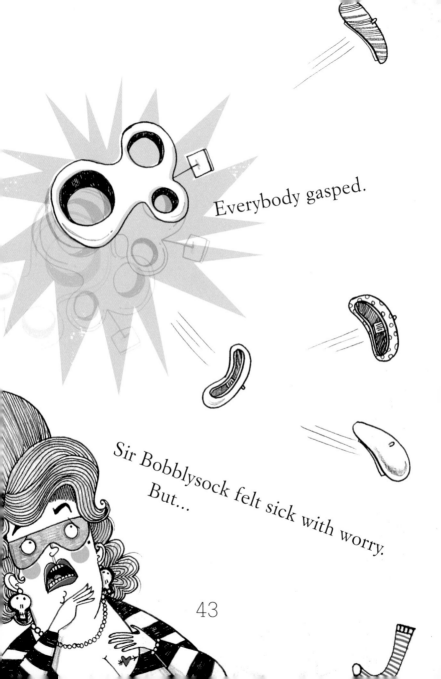

Everybody gasped.

Sir Bobblysock felt sick with worry. But...

43

...Claude saved the day!

Soon the Mayor arrived.
'Claude you are a hero!' he cried.

He gave Claude a medal and
whisked him and Sir Bobblysock
off for a slap-up dinner.

Back in the kitchen of Mr and Mrs Shinyshoes' house, Claude and Sir Bobblysock snuggled down in their beds. Claude closed his beady eyes.

A little later on, Mr and Mrs Shinyshoes came home from work.

'Where on earth has this medal come from?' asked Mrs Shinyshoes. 'Do you know anything about this, Claude?'

'Look, he's fast asleep!' laughed Mr Shinyshoes. 'We'll have to find out in the morning.'

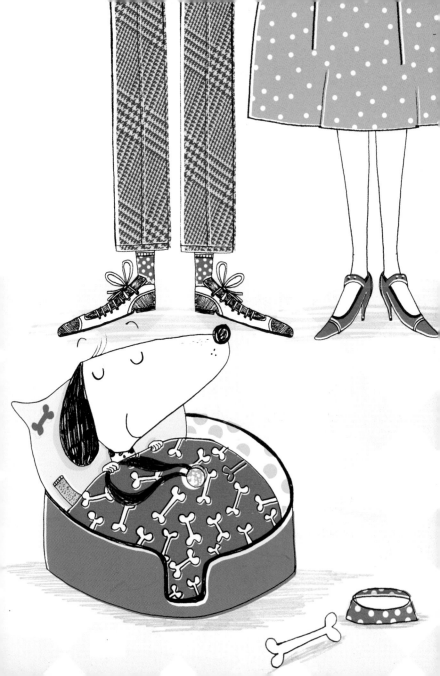

# Part II

But the next morning, Mr and Mrs Shinyshoes had already gone to work by the time Claude woke up.

He looked around for Sir Bobblysock, who often helped him put on his beret.

He would do this very importantly, as it was a very important job.

That morning, however, Sir
Bobblysock did not do his job
very importantly.

In fact, he didn't do it at all.
He just lay in bed like a sad, sick sock.

Claude looked at him very closely and frowned.

Sir Bobblysock did have the habit of sometimes pretending to be poorly.

He would lie there, all cross-eyed and floppy, waiting for Claude to find him and make a big fuss.

'Hmm...' said Claude, and he poked Sir Bobblysock in the tummy.

'Hmm...' he said again, and he prodded Sir Bobblysock's bobbles.

'Hmm...' he said for the third time, and he took Sir Bobblysock's temperature with a banana.

Claude thought for a minute.
'Sir Bobblysock,' he said, 'you are
not very well. All that shopping and
rushing around in the city has worn
you out. I think I will have to take
you to the hospital!'

So he did.

Claude didn't know where to find an ambulance, so instead he decided to make his own.

He tucked Sir Bobblysock safely under his arm and put on his rollerskates.

Flashing his torch above his head
and shouting 'Woo! Woo! Woo!' for
the siren, he skated to the hospital
with Sir Bobblysock.

They arrived in no time at all.

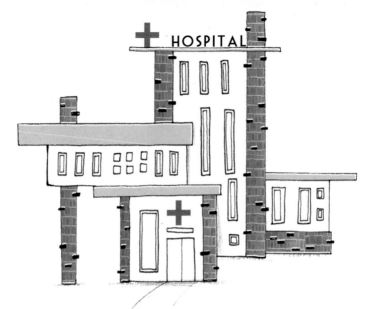

The hospital was a tall white
building which smelt of medicine
and sticky plasters.

Claude had only ever seen pictures
of hospitals in books before. He
thought that a real one was much
better, because it wasn't flat and
drawn on paper.

Claude popped Sir Bobblysock in a
wheelchair. They joined the end of a
long queue of people, all waiting to
see the doctor.

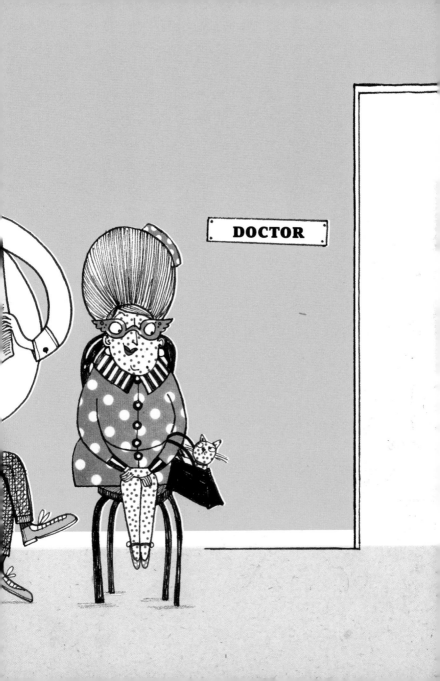

Claude didn't mind waiting because he had a tail to wag, but Sir Bobblysock grumbled until Claude got him a cup of milk and a biscuit to dunk.

Eventually it was time for Sir Bobblysock to see the doctor. He was a tall, thin man with a tidy moustache and something dangling around his neck.

'I am Dr Ivan Achinbum,' he said. 'What seems to be the problem?'

Sir Bobblysock suddenly came over
all shy, so Claude explained.

'I see...' said Dr Achinbum.
'Well, we will soon get you feeling
better again. Now let me
have a look at you.'

Claude watched closely as Dr Achinbum prodded and poked Sir Bobblysock's tummy, listened to his heart with the dangly thing and took Sir Bobblysock's temperature (this time with a thermometer, not a banana).

Claude sniffed haughtily. He ALWAYS found bananas were much better for taking temperatures.

Dr Achinbum wrinkled his brow
and looked at Claude.

'I need to take your friend for an
X-ray so we can see what's going on
inside him. You stay here and we
will be back soon.'

And he wheeled Sir Bobblysock out
of the room in his wheelchair.

Claude was now alone in the room.
At first he sat very still.

Then his eyes started to wander.
Then his paws, and then his body.

He started to look through all the
drawers and cupboards.

There were bandages and sticky plasters and safety pins and lots of other exciting things besides.

Last of all he opened a tall cupboard… and gasped.

He gasped like this: GASP!

There, hanging all alone, was a
white coat exactly like the ones
Dr Achinbum and the other doctors
were wearing.

Claude reached in, took the coat off
the hanger and put it on.

'I look just like a doctor!' he said
and he twirled around to see
himself from every side.

Just then the door burst
open and a tall nurse
rushed in, looking
red-faced and
bothered.

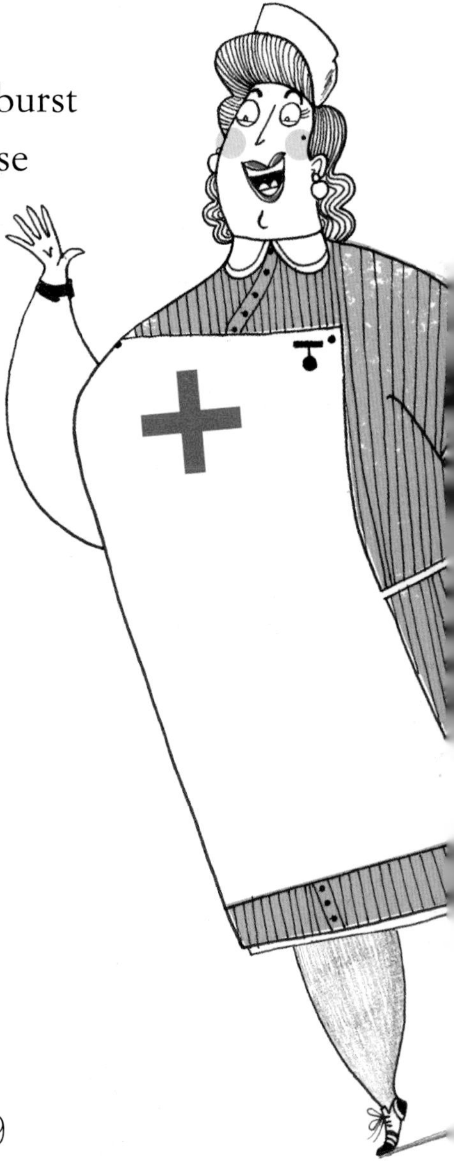

'Oh, Doctor!'
she cried. 'Thank
goodness I've
found you!'

Claude looked around to find the
doctor she was talking to, but there
was no one else in the room.

She was talking to HIM!

'There's an emergency!' the nurse
said, and with a deep breath she
told him all about it.

71

Apparently, a group of wrestlers had come into the hospital all complaining of a mystery illness – and now everyone in the waiting room had caught it!

The nurse said that Claude was the only doctor she could find. He would have to find out what this mysterious illness was.

Before Claude could explain that he
wasn't a real doctor – he was just
Claude – the enormous nurse had
hauled him into the waiting room.

Well, everyone was in a terrible state.

The wrestlers were groaning in the corner. A large man covered in tattoos had dropped his embroidery and was fainting by the pot plant. And some acrobats from the circus that had come to town were lying over the front desk.

ELP DES

Claude had no idea what
to do! He tried to remember
when he had been poorly.

There was the time he had been to
an 'All you can eat' restaurant and
had eaten everything, including his
table.

He had been sick the next morning.
Maybe these people in the waiting
room had done the same.

But nobody smelt of noodles or
plywood so that wasn't the problem.

77

Claude scratched his head.

Once, he had tried to knit a deckchair and ended up tying himself in knots, so he'd fallen over and bumped his head. He took a quick look around the waiting room.

No one had any knitting needles and nobody's head was bright-red and bumpy.

No, that wasn't the problem.

Claude sighed. There was only one thing for it.

He rummaged around in his beret until he found an emergency banana. He then started to take people's temperatures with it.

But by the time he'd finished, he still didn't know what the problem was.

Nobody was too hot and nobody was too cold.

Claude was just wondering if he should start prodding people, when there came a noise from behind the desk.

Bong! Bong! Bong! Bong! Bong! Bong! Bong! Bong! Bong! Bong! Bong!

It was the clock striking eleven o'clock in the morning.

Suddenly Claude felt himself starting to wobble! He felt like he was about to faint.

And it was exactly then that he realised what the mystery illness was.

'Nurse!' he cried, 'I've solved the problem! These people have got eleven-o'clock-itis! What they need is a nice cup of tea and a sit down. And possibly a biscuit, if you have any?'

The nurse beamed a big smile, spun around (Claude ducked) and clattered off to the kitchen.

She came back carrying a huge tray piled high with cups and biscuits, and a gigantic teapot.

Claude helped her dish out the drinks and biscuits to the people in the waiting room.

As soon as they had dunked their biscuits and had a slurp of tea they started to come round.

It wasn't very long before the wrestlers had each other in headlocks,

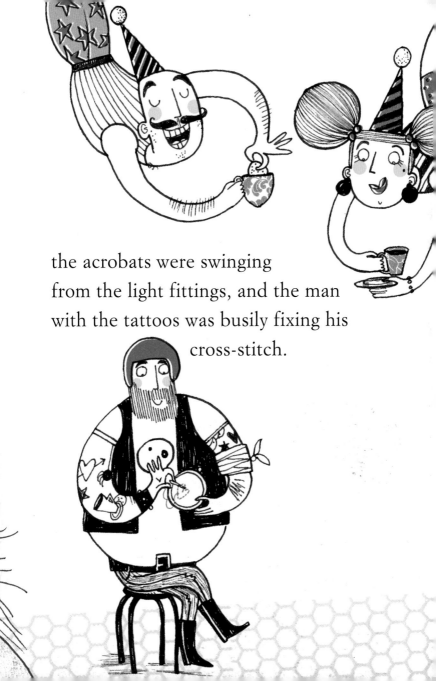

the acrobats were swinging
from the light fittings, and the man
with the tattoos was busily fixing his
cross-stitch.

In the distance Claude could hear Dr Achinbum talking to Sir Bobblysock, so he ran back to the office.

Claude took off the Doctor's coat and hung it up in the cupboard.

88

Then he quickly combed his ears
with a clipboard and sat down
neatly in the chair.

Seconds later, Dr Achinbum
arrived, wheeling Sir Bobblysock –
who, Claude thought, looked
a lot better.

'He's all better!' said Dr Achinbum to Claude. 'We've solved the problem. He had a small hole in the heel, so we've had our best surgeon darn it and now he's as good as new!'

Claude was going to ask if Sir Bobblysock had behaved himself, but then he noticed that his friend was wearing a large sticker which said, 'I was DARN good in hospital,' so he didn't bother.

'You are free to go home now!' said
Dr Achinbum.

So Claude said "thank you" and
"goodbye" and set off with Sir
Bobblysock...

but they didn't go by ambulance.

The wrestlers were so grateful to
Claude for curing them of the
mystery illness that they carried
him and Sir Bobblysock all the
way home.

Claude and Sir Bobblysock decided this was a very good way to travel.

Only perhaps not every day…

Next time you are in the city or at the hospital see if your beady eye can spot a:

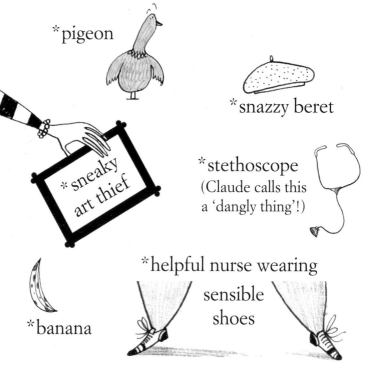

*pigeon

*snazzy beret

*sneaky art thief

*stethoscope
(Claude calls this a 'dangly thing'!)

*helpful nurse wearing sensible shoes

*banana

And remember to keep your eyes out for Claude and Sir Bobblysock. You never know where they might pop up next!